ZOMBIE REPELLENT

ZOMBIE REPEL

© 2017 MARVEL

First published by Scholastic Australia in 2015.
This edition published by Scholastic Australia in 2017.

Scholastic Australia Pty Limited
PO Box 579 Gosford NSW 2250
ABN 11 000 614 577
www.scholastic.com.au

Part of the Scholastic Group

Sydney • Auckland • New York • Toronto • London • Mexico City • New Delhi • Hong Kong • Buenos Aires • Puerto Rico

ISBN 978-1-74276-604-1

Printed in China by RR Donnelley.

Scholastic Australia's policy, in association with RR Donnelley, is to use papers that are renewable and made efficiently from wood grown in responsibly managed forests, so as to minimise its environmental footprint.

10 9 8 7 6 5 4 3 2 1   17 18 19 20 21 / 1

LENT

STARRING

ANT-MAN

BY CHRIS "DOC" WYATT

ILLUSTRATED BY

KHOI PHAM AND CHRIS SOTOMAYOR

SCHOLASTIC

SYDNEY AUCKLAND NEW YORK TORONTO LONDON MEXICO CITY
NEW DELHI HONG KONG BUENOS AIRES PUERTO RICO

FEATURING YOUR FAVOURITES!

ANT-MAN

EUCLID

CAPTAIN AMERICA

IRON MAN

HULK

BRUCE BANNER

HAWKEYE

BLACK WIDOW

FALCON

THOR

HELICARRIER

ROBOT

THE LIVING UNDEAD

ANT ZOMBIES

COUNT NEFARIA

ZOMBIE VIRUS

THE STORY OF ANT-MAN

*L*ife has never been easy for **Scott Lang**, an electronics expert who was forced into a career of crime to help his family. Scott always regretted breaking the law and only wanted to do what was right.

One day, the famous scientist **Dr. Hank Pym** reached out to Scott and provided a way for him to put an end to his life of crime.

Using gear invented by Dr. Pym, Scott became the Astonishing Ant-Man, a hero capable of shrinking to the size of an ant, with the power of a hundred men.

Dr. Pym's technology revolves around the use of **"Pym Particles"**—an unusual set of subatomic particles capable of reducing the mass of any object. Scott, using the Pym Particles, has the ability to shrink not only himself, but also anyone or anything else. Using the Pym Particles, he can even sometimes enlarge things.

Pym Particles

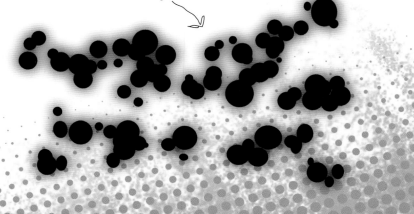

In addition, Scott can use other technology to communicate with ants and even summon them when they might be helpful. Since he's an electronics expert, Scott is continually modifying and expanding Dr. Pym's equipment, making it his own.

A dedicated hero, Scott Lang has put his past far behind him. Now he fights crime and protects the innocent as the Astonishing

CHAPTER 1

It was a beautiful day in New York City, and Central Park was filled with the regular crowds. There were tourists strolling around, taking pictures. There were joggers steadily exercising their way down the footpaths. There were picnickers, kids on school excursions and artists painting landscapes. There were even a few celebrities, keeping their collars up and sunglasses on, hoping not to get noticed.

And yet almost none of the hundreds of people walking around the park even thought about the fact that there was a whole other world beneath their feet—the world of the

INSECTS!

Millions of insects made the dirt under Central Park their home and on a nice warm day like this one, the bugs were even busier than the humans were!

There was, however, one person who was paying very close attention to the insects and he didn't like what he saw.

"That's strange," said **Scott Lang**, the Astonishing Ant-Man, as he crouched to examine the tracks made by some ants that had recently passed through. "These aren't the traffic patterns I would expect," he mumbled to himself.

Of course, it was easier for Ant-Man to notice what the insects were up to because of his amazing power. He had the ability to **shrink to the *SIZE* of an ant!**

Right then he was no bigger than a bug, and he was standing in the tunnel entrance of an anthill.

"I need to find out what's happening," Scott said to himself as he followed the ant tracks deeper down the tunnel. To better understand ants, Ant-Man had been studying their behaviour up close for years. He'd come to that particular anthill several times. And he could tell that something just wasn't right.

When he reached one of the anthill's main chambers, he was surprised to find most members of the ant colony lined up in a perfect row, standing at attention like little soldiers.

"What are you doing, guys?" Ant-Man asked out loud. Usually there was as much commotion in one of these chambers as in a New York subway station during rush hour, so it was eerie to see all the ants standing completely still. **"Are you sick or something?"**

Of course, ants didn't understand English, but Ant-Man did have the ability to communicate with them. Ant-Man's equipment could release **pheromone scents**. Ants, which had a much stronger sense of smell than humans did, used those kinds of odours to send messages to one another.

But even when Ant-Man released pheromones, the ants still didn't respond; they just stood there in a trance. They weren't asleep, but it wasn't like they were fully awake, either!

"I have to get to the bottom of this," said Ant-Man as he used a syringe to get a sample of an ant's **hemolymph**, the clear fluid ants had instead of blood.

Ant-Man stuck the sample in his handheld device, which clicked and beeped before flashing a report across its screen.

"A VIRUS?" said Ant-Man, reading from the device. "I've never seen this kind before, but according to these readings, I suspect it **could be passed to humans!**

"This could be extremely serious," said Ant-Man, "like the time that space virus quickly ripped through a **S.H.I.E.L.D.** moon base. All one hundred and twenty agents were infected within hours!"

The space station incident had been different, because the station was contained, so the virus couldn't spread to Earth. Ant-Man didn't even want to think about what could happen if some unknown virus started to infect people across New York City. It could quickly become an epidemic that could get millions of people sick . . . or worse!

Ant-Man knew immediately that he had to take his information to the best Super Hero team in the world. **"I have to find the Avengers,"** said Ant-Man. "I might be able to research a cure for this by myself, but if the virus starts to spread, it will take a whole team to manage containment. The Avengers will know what to do!"

Ant-Man rushed from the anthill . . . but as soon as he was gone, the ants he had been examining started to move.

Reaching the surface, Ant-Man sized himself up to his normal human height and rushed off to find Iron Man and the other Avengers.

As he left, he passed a couple picnicking on a blanket in the grass.

"Boy, the ants really are out today," said the man.

"Yeah, they're everywhere," agreed the woman. **"Ouch! I think one just bit me . . ."**

CHAPTER 2

*I*t was easy for Ant-Man to find the Avengers. All he had to do was follow the sound of explosions and look for plumes of smoke. The heroes were clearly in the middle of a big battle.

"That way, Euclid!" Ant-Man said to the giant flying ant he was riding.

Not only did Ant-Man have the ability to shrink himself to the size of an ant; he also had the power to enlarge ants to human scale.

Whenever he needed to get across the city quickly, he used a pheromone scent to summon **Euclid**, his favourite ant friend, and hitch a ride.

"The Avengers are fighting the Maggia," Ant-Man said as Euclid landed on the wall of a building that looked down on the block where the entire Avengers team was engaged in combat with the criminals.

The Maggia, a criminal organisation under the control of the evil villain Count Nefaria, had been caught red-handed breaking into a S.H.I.E.L.D. warehouse that held many experimental weapons, but it looked like the fight was almost over. The Hulk was holding down four Maggia soldiers, Thor had knocked out several others, and an energy cage built by Falcon held most of the rest.

"Face it, Count," shouted Captain America to Nefaria, **"this little heist attempt has failed!"**

"The Maggia never give up!" yelled back Nefaria as he used a laser rifle to blow a hole through the warehouse wall and dash inside.

"Oh, no!" shouted Iron Man, who knew

what kind of weapons were stored in that warehouse. "Grab him before he can get the—"

BOOM!

It was too late! A giant robot, piloted by **Count Nefaria**, burst through the warehouse wall, firing a barrage of missiles at the Avengers!

THANKS TO THIS S.H.I.E.L.D. ROBOTIC MECH-ARMOUR, NOTHING CAN STOP ME NOW!

Seeing all this, Ant-Man knew he needed to help. "Get me down there, Euclid," he said, and Euclid took off toward the battle scene.

As Nefaria's missiles blasted Hawkeye and Cap, Hulk leapt to his feet. **"HULK SMASH!"** he shouted as he charged like a steam train at the giant robot.

"I don't think so!" shouted Nefaria, using the robot's claws to bat Hulk away. **Hulk went sailing through the air!**

Hawkeye shot explosive arrows and **Thor** aimed bolts of lightning at the robot, but it still kept coming, knocking back **Cap** and **Black Widow!**

"How do we stop it?" Hawkeye shouted to Iron Man.

"I'm not sure," Iron Man replied. "It's based on my own designs and I'm a pretty great designer! Maybe it doesn't have any weaknesses."

At that moment, **Nefaria** reached out with the robot's arms and plucked **Falcon** out of the sky, then slammed him to the ground!

The robot raised its giant foot, ready to CRUSH HIM!

"Say hello to Ant-Man!" Ant-Man replied as he grew larger from out of nowhere. He was right behind the count, inside the robot's cockpit!

"What? Who?"

asked a confused **Count Nefaria** as Ant-Man knocked him back into the robot's controls.

Falcon and the other Avengers peered through the robot's cockpit window, shocked to see Ant-Man inside. They had no idea that Ant-Man, shrunk down to a tiny size, had been able to slip into the robot's armour through an exhaust vent. Climbing along the robot's cables, he'd made his way into the cockpit, where he had grown to normal size and attacked Nefaria!

After knocking the villain out, Ant-Man shut the robot down and opened the cockpit. Then he threw Nefaria to the ground at the Avengers' feet.

"Thanks," said Falcon as Ant-Man climbed down from the robot.

"Good work, soldier," Cap said, patting Ant-Man on the back.

"So they do have a weakness," observed Iron Man as he examined the unpowered robot's exhaust vent. "I'll have to work on the design more."

"If your design was any better, I don't know if we would have survived," Black Widow told Iron Man.

Hawkeye walked up to Ant-Man. "Thanks for the assist and everything, bug-boy, but what are you doing here?"

"Right! I can't believe I forgot. **I have vital information!**" Ant-Man said urgently, taking out a high-tech device.

CHAPTER 3

"You're showing us ant blood?" asked Hawkeye, confused.

"I'm showing you an image of the virus," replied Ant-Man, pointing to the scan on his handheld device.

"What did this . . . virus do to the ants?" asked Captain America.

"They weren't acting like themselves," replied Ant-Man. "They weren't moving around."

"Maybe they're just lazy ants," Hawkeye said, shrugging.

"No, it was like they were in a trance," replied Ant-Man. It didn't seem like the Avengers understood how dangerous the virus could be. "In tropical areas, there's a fungal infection that ants can get. This fungus turns them into *ZOMBIE ANTS*. My worry is that this virus might act like that fungus."

Hawkeye snorted. **"Zombie ants?"**

"It's real," protested Ant-Man. "Look it up."

"Can this virus spread to humans?" asked Falcon.

"It looks like it," Ant-Man responded.

Hawkeye sneered. "But you don't know for sure?"

Ant-Man shrugged. *"No."*

"This is all very interesting, but I'm going to have to cut it short," interrupted Iron Man. "I just got a call from Jarvis. A.I.M. is attacking in Battery Park. We have to get down there . . . **AVENGERS, ASSEMBLE!**" he shouted.

The Avengers dashed off, leaving Ant-Man alone. Ant-Man knew that if A.I.M., an organisation of **evil geniuses**, was up to no good, then the Avengers had to respond. But he'd thought they would help him with the virus problem, and they didn't even seem to believe him. "It's like they weren't even listening to me," complained Ant-Man.

Ant-Man turned to see a man in tattered clothes standing nearby. It took a second for Ant-Man to realise that it was **Dr. Bruce Banner**, the world-renowned scientist.

Behind him, many **S.H.I.E.L.D.** agents were arriving to clean up the aftermath of the fight.

"Bruce, it's you. I thought you would still be the . . . *other guy*," said Scott, referring to the **Incredible Hulk**, whom Banner transformed into when he grew angry.

"Sometimes he calms down quickly after a battle, and then . . . I come back," explained Banner. "But tell me about this insect virus you discovered."

"I thought it was important, but the other Avengers didn't seem to think it was . . . so maybe it isn't," said Scott.

"Always trust your instincts, Scott," said Banner. "Even if others don't believe in you, you should believe in yourself. Especially if those instincts could save lives."

Scott nodded, understanding. He knew Banner was right. Working by himself, Scott sometimes felt unimportant, but Banner's words gave him a spark of confidence.

"So, what kind of virus is it?" asked Banner.

"Here, see for yourself," said Scott, handing Banner his device.

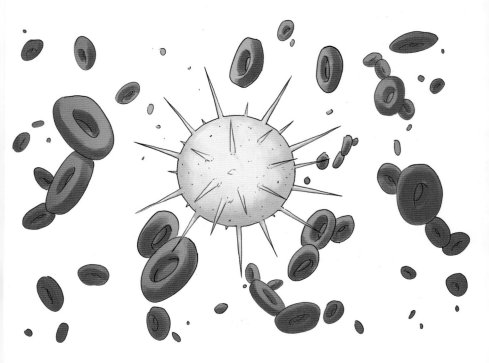

"Hmmm . . . you got any samples?" asked Banner as he studied the data.

"Sure," said Scott. "Why?"

"There are a few more tests we should do," Banner replied. **"Come back to my lab."**

Banner's private lab was onboard a **S.H.I.E.L.D.** floating fortress called the **Helicarrier.** Scott had never been on the giant airship and was excited to be there, but that excitement turned to concern as Banner showed him the new test results.

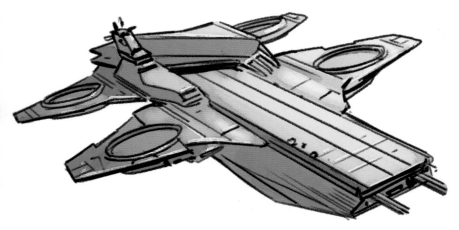

Banner wasn't an expert on disease, but he knew a lot about blood reactions because of his work in **gamma radiation**.

"Great, that's the last thing we need," said Banner, "a bunch of living undead making their way around Manhattan like a **B-GRADE HORROR MOVIE**. I need to let the others know how serious this is."

Banner called the communicator in Iron Man's helmet. Every Avenger had one of these **"comm units"** in or near one of their ears so they could easily coordinate with one another, even from different locations during battle.

"Little busy, Bruce," Iron Man responded over the sound of laser fire.

"I'm here with Ant-Man," Banner responded. "That virus of his? It's a **BIG** deal."

"Even if it is, we can't deal with it right now. We're under heavy fire!" Iron Man shouted. "These A.I.M. guys are acting strangely—more viciously than usual! And they just keep coming!"

"Iron Man, this disease could become a massive outbreak unless—" But Banner wasn't able to finish his thought, because he was interrupted by the sound of an explosion.

"Gonna have to call you back," said Iron Man as he cut communications.

Banner levelled a significant look at Scott.

"Well, for now, we're on our own," he said.

CHAPTER 4

"**I**'ve been with the Avengers for a while now," Banner shouted to Ant-Man over the rush of the wind. "In that time I've done a lot of strange things. I've fought alien creatures from space. I've visited other planets and helped defend a city of people who live under the ocean. . . And yet I can honestly say this is one of the strangest things I've ever done."

Banner was saying this while clutching
tightly to Euclid's back. When Ant-Man and
Banner realised that the other Avengers weren't
able to help, they decided to head back to
Central Park to re-examine the infected ants,
hoping there would be a way to develop
a cure. All the **S.H.I.E.L.D.**
shuttles were currently in use,
so Ant-Man suggested they
fly on the back of his
ant friend.

"You get used to it," Ant-Man shouted. "And thank you for believing me when no-one else did."

"Sure," said Banner. "I don't know why the others didn't pay enough attention."

"I do," Ant-Man replied. "It's me. I talk to bugs and I shrink. Those aren't really super powers. I mean, they are kind of, I guess. But Thor's a near-immortal Asgardian, Captain America's a legendary Super-Soldier, and Iron Man has more firepower than a small army. Hawkeye and Black Widow don't have powers, but they have years of super-spy experience with S.H.I.E.L.D. And what do I have? Bugs!

If I were them, I don't think I'd take me very seriously, either. Let's face it, I'm no big strong hero like the Hulk."

"You think people look up to the Hulk?" Banner asked sharply. "When I become the Hulk, people only think of me as a monster. The Hulk is a hero and wants to help. But people don't understand that. They run from him, even when he's trying to save them. Everything runs from the Hulk.

"And it's not just when I'm Hulk—it's when I'm Bruce Banner, too," he continued. "Even when I'm human, some people still think of me as a monster. I went to a conference last month to present some of my research, but no-one listened to my presentation. They spent the whole time worrying about making me angry."

Ant-Man knew what Banner meant. It was difficult being misjudged by people who hadn't gotten to know you yet.

"I started to correspond with some other electronics specialists I met online," Ant-Man said to Banner. "We traded ideas, brainstormed new inventions, that kind of thing. But when they found out I was a Super Hero, things got awkward. They stopped talking to me. I guess it was all just too strange for them."

Banner nodded, understanding, but their conversation was interrupted as Euclid came in for a landing. Ant-Man used his Pym Particle gun to shrink himself and Banner, but when they went into the same anthill Ant-Man had investigated a few hours earlier, all the ants were gone.

"That's really strange," Ant-Man said. "Usually there are at least some ants left to guard the tunnels. It's like this place has been completely abandoned."

When the two left the anthill and enlarged back to human size, Banner looked around. **"Hey, where is everybody?"**

Ant-Man saw what Banner meant. When he had been there earlier, the park had been busy, packed with hundreds of people . . . Now there was no-one.

"Look at this,"

Ant-Man said to Banner, pointing at a picnic blanket that had been abandoned. "The sandwiches are half eaten, as if these people left right in the middle of their lunch."

"There are some people," Banner said, spotting across the park a crowd standing with their backs to the heroes. When Ant-Man and Banner got closer, the people turned on them and **SNARLED!**

Ant-Man was shocked!

Something was horribly wrong! Everyone in

the group had webs of pulsing blue veins bulging out all over their pale-green-tinted skin! Their eyes were a sickly mucous yellow and had no pupils!

"What happened to them?" asked Banner urgently.

"The undead virus! They've been infected!" shouted Ant-Man. **"They have become the—**

their teeth! "This makes me miss hanging out with insects!" Ant-Man shouted as he dodged their bites.

CHAPTER 5

*T*hese "living undead" didn't move slowly, like zombies in old movies. Their arms and legs were stiff, but they could move very *fast!* In no time, the undead had Ant-Man and Banner backed up against a cluster of trees.

"Don't let them bite you!" warned Ant-Man, trying to push the undead off him. "You'll get infected, too."

44

"What can we do?" asked Banner. "We don't want to hurt them. They're not bad guys, just sick humans. We have to help them!"

But as the undead roared and scratched at him, Banner felt himself getting angry . . . and starting to change.

Ant-Man looked at his friend. Oh, no! If Banner changed into Hulk, Hulk might lash out against his attackers, hurting them—or much worse. Ant-Man had only seconds to figure out how to stop Banner from changing . . .

That was when he spotted something on the ground he could use to solve the problem. To anyone else, this thing wouldn't have seemed like much, but because of Ant-Man's particular skills, it was exactly what was needed.

It was an earthworm.

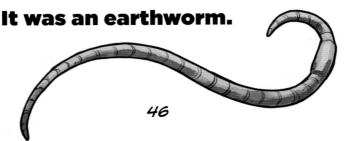

Ant-Man dodged the grabbing hands of the living undead and snatched up the worm.

Quickly, he tossed it between the undead and Banner, then **enlarged it!**

The earthworm was suddenly **huge**, and it became a living wall, with Ant-Man and Banner on one side and the living undead on the other!

"**Are you okay, Bruce?**" asked Ant-Man, putting an arm around the scientist.

"Yeah," Banner assured him, calming down. His transformation stopped. "But what do we do now?"

They could hear frustrated howls coming from the other side of the earthworm.

"**I'll call Euclid,**" Ant-Man said as he released a pheromone scent. "We have something to show the other Avengers now."

"**We do?**" asked Banner.

Ant-Man pointed to his wrist, where a small wearable camera was mounted. "I got it all on video!"

Back inside Banner's lab aboard the **S.H.I.E.L.D.** Helicarrier, Scott uploaded the video files to the Avengers' server. Out in the field, the Avengers were able to use their handheld devices to stream the footage of the living undead attacking Scott and Bruce.

"I am sorry I didn't take this more seriously," said Iron Man grimly. He and the other Avengers were still in Battery Park, having just stopped the **A.I.M.** attack.

"How far has it spread?" asked Black Widow.

"We don't know exactly," Banner said to them over comms. "But **S.H.I.E.L.D.** is starting to get alarm calls from midtown. That seems to be the epicentre. We're in the lab now, because there's a chance that Scott and I can work up a cure."

"We've already got most of the materials we need," said Scott, "but the virus is spreading already. The Avengers can help by trying to find the infected civilians and quarantining them so they can't bite more people!"

"Look, you may have been the first person to find this virus," said Hawkeye, "but that doesn't mean you get to tell us what we should be doing—"

Captain America cut off Hawkeye's comment before the archer could even finish his thought.

"We understand," Captain America said directly to Scott. "We Avengers will head to Central Park and try to separate the living undead from people who haven't been infected. We want to stop the spread of this thing."

"It could already have gone further than we think," said Iron Man seriously. "It might explain the behaviour of these A.I.M. agents. We can't see their faces, because of the A.I.M. uniform masks. But they were fighting strangely, just like those living undead in Scott's video."

"If those A.I.M. guys are infected, then be careful that you don't get infected, too," warned

Scott. "It spreads through bites."

"We'll be fine," Hawkeye assured Ant-Man. "Like Iron Man said, the A.I.M. guys are wearing masks, so they can't bite us."

"Yes, but something must have bitten them to infect them in the first place," Scott pointed out.

"He's right. Everyone, check your skin and clothes. Make sure no ants have gotten on you," warned Cap.

"Watch out!"

Falcon called, spotting an ant on Iron Man, but it slipped between two metal armour plates before Falcon could reach it.

"Don't worry, this isn't the first time I've had a 'bug' in my

"systems," Iron Man joked as he quickly pulled off pieces of armour, trying to get to the ant. Despite what he was saying, Iron Man was clearly a little freaked out.

"Uh-oh," said Iron Man. "I'm . . . feeling STRANGE..." Then he dropped to the ground!

Falcon rushed to his side and scanned for the ant where Tony had removed part of his armour. **"Gotcha,"** said Falcon as he crushed the infected ant . . . but it was too late. The ant had already bitten **Iron Man!**

Iron Man's limbs grew stiff and he started to moan.

"Tony? Tony? Can you still hear me?" asked Falcon. He got no response, but Iron Man started to aim his repulsors at the others.

"Scatter!"

Cap commanded as Iron Man fired at him and the others. All the Avengers dove for cover!

On the Helicarrier, Scott and Banner could only listen, horrified, as the undead Iron Man blasted at his teammates!

CHAPTER 6

*B*anner and Scott listened anxiously on comms to everything that was happening in Battery Park. Captain America, Black Widow, Hawkeye, Thor and Falcon scattered, avoiding the repulsor blasts from the undead Iron Man!

"We have to take Iron Man down without hurting him," shouted Cap as he raised his shield to deflect one of the blasts. "Even alone, an undead Iron Man could destroy half the city. We have to give Ant-Man and Bruce time to come up with a cure."

"My lightning will slow him down!" Thor said as he spun his war hammer, Mjolnir, in the air. Lightning shot from the hammer, slamming into Iron Man.

"No, Thor! Wait!" shouted Falcon . . . but it was too late!

The lightning hit Iron Man, then blasted straight

back out of him, pounding Thor to the ground!

Falcon quickly explained to the astonished Avengers, "Tony insulated the armour, designing it to be able to redirect lightning strikes!"

As Iron Man zapped the ground around the other Avengers, everyone ducked and rolled to safety.

"Did you see the raw power of that blast?" asked Widow. "It's like the lightning has supercharged Tony's armour!"

"Oh, great!" shouted Hawkeye, sarcastically. "With Thor down, what can we do?"

In his lab on the Helicarrier, a worried Banner looked urgently at Scott. **"We have to get down there and help!"**

"No, we can't help anyone until

we find a cure for this **ZOMBIE virus!**" Scott replied.

"There's got to be something we can do," said Banner.

"There is," said Scott. "I can send a friend."

Only minutes later, undead Iron Man almost had Cap, Falcon and Widow cornered when they heard Ant-Man's voice: "Sorry about this, Iron Man, but you'll thank me once you're back to your old self!"

Confused about the source of Ant-Man's voice, the heroes looked up just as an ant the size of a truck slammed into Iron Man, knocking him away!

"Now I've seen everything!" shouted Hawkeye.

But when the ant turned back to them, they could see a video screen strapped to its head. On-screen, Ant-Man explained:

LOOK, I'M STILL IN THE LAB WITH DR. BANNER, BUT WE SENT THIS GUY TO HELP.

It was Ant-Man's ant friend **Euclid**. Ant-Man had increased its size even more than usual and then strapped some gear to him, including the video screen. "I have a pheromone box attached to his harness," Ant-Man said. "I can send him scent messages remotely in order to communicate with him and control what he does."

Undead Iron Man swung back around, and Euclid wasted no time jumping into the fight with him. Iron Man's repulsor blasts bounced off the energy deflectors Ant-Man had built into the ant's harness. Euclid then charged at Iron Man.

"I never expected to say this," said Cap, **"but come on, everyone, let's give that ant some backup!"**

In the lab, Scott watched on the screen as Euclid and the Avengers battled undead Iron Man. Then he turned back to his work with Dr. Banner.

"This last batch might be the solution we need. Let's check," said Banner, using an eyedropper to put some chemicals on a slide, then examining the results under a microscope.

As Banner watched, the chemicals attacked the sample viruses on the microscope slide.

"It seems to be working," Banner said, but then added, **"Wait, wait. . . No . . ."**

To Banner's disappointment, each of the sample viruses was able to repel the chemicals.

"It's as if the cure wants to work but has trouble bonding with the virus," complained a frustrated Banner.

"**Hmmm . . .** This all started with the ants in Central Park," Scott said. "Maybe the virus is more adapted to ant physiology. Let's try using ant hemolymph as the bonding agent!"

"**Brilliant,**" said Banner. Quickly the two men prepared another slide and stuck it under the microscope. Peering through the lens, Banner watched as the new version of the cure killed all the sample viruses on the slide.

"We did it!" shouted Banner, excited.

"Well, it works in the lab, anyway," said Scott. **"But now we're going to need to test it on humans."**

"For that we'll need a test subject," Banner said. "We're going to have to catch one of the living undead and bring it back here."

"Oh, I got your test subject right here," said Hawkeye as he and Cap entered the lab, carrying an unconscious Tony Stark between them.

"With Euclid's help we were able to knock Iron Man out," said Cap. **"If there's a chance you can cure Tony, we need to take it."**

"All right," agreed Scott. "Let's get him up on the table, remove his armour and hope that we can turn him back to normal."

CHAPTER 7

"**A**re you sure we have to do this?" asked Banner.

Cap and Hawkeye watched as Banner and Scott prepped to test the cure on Tony Stark. The other Avengers were out in the streets, doing their best to protect bystanders from the growing crowds of infected people who were turning into the living undead.

"I'm sorry, Doctor, but we do,"
Scott replied. "If we're going to mass produce the cure, we're going to need to take readings from the moment the chemicals first touch the virus. In this lab, we don't have instruments sensitive enough to get those readings from outside his body. With what we have available, the only way I know how to do it is to literally shrink someone down and send him in with the cure. So I will use my Pym Particles to micro-size you, then inject you into Tony's bloodstream."

"Me?" asked Banner, surprised.

"Yes," confirmed Scott. "As you deliver the cure to the virus, you'll also operate a probe to take the readings. Remember: we need that data if we want to have any hope of helping New York!"

"You have to send someone else," insisted Banner. "Being inside Tony, curing him, getting the vital readings . . . that is a lot of pressure. If something pushes me over the edge, I could turn into the Hulk . . ."

Scott nodded grimly. He knew exactly what could happen if a confused and angry Hulk rampaged through Tony Stark's bloodstream. Imagine having a tiny Hulk swim into your heart . . . not a pretty picture.

"Bruce is right. Send one of us," suggested Cap, referring to Hawkeye and himself.

"I wish I could," Scott said. "But you two don't know how to work the probe. Neither do I. I understand the electrical systems, but it requires specialised operation that I've just never trained for. Dr. Banner uses this probe all the time in his gamma research. It has to be him."

Cap, Banner and Hawkeye all shared uncomfortable looks.

Scott sighed, then looked at Banner. "I understand why you're uncomfortable, but, Dr. Banner, earlier you told me I needed to believe in myself. Well, now it's your turn to do just that. You can do this . . . You have to."

Banner looked at Scott and knew he was right. He nodded. "Okay," the scientist said. "If we're really going to do this, let's move quickly. The undead virus must be spreading through the city like wildfire."

Working quickly, Banner got suited up in breathing gear and Scott shrank him and a canister of the new cure down to microscopic size using his Pym Particles. Then Scott injected Banner right into Tony Stark's arm.

Dr. Banner had been to a lot of strange places as an Avenger: an antimatter universe called the Negative Zone, a subatomic dimension called the Microverse and a couple of different possible future Earths. He'd even ridden on a flying ant named Euclid with Scott! And he'd thought that was as weird as it got. Nope, Tony's bloodstream was definitely the weirdest place of all.

"**Where am I headed?**" Banner asked Scott via his comm.

"Just move forward—there should be copies of the virus all through his blood," Scott replied.

Suddenly, a small round white object slammed into Banner, knocking him back.

"**What was that?**" he asked.

"It must have been one of Tony's white blood cells," Scott said. "Tony's immune system thinks you're a disease."

"**Not pleasant,**" said Dr. Banner. "I hope more aren't coming my way."

He looked up to see that, yes, more were coming—a lot more! Within seconds Banner was getting pelted by tons of white blood cells, as if a couple of teams of vicious dodgeball players were letting loose on him. He was being battered and beaten!

"You've got to help me!" Banner called to Scott.

Scott could hear by the tone of Banner's voice that he was getting angry: he was only moments away from turning into the Hulk!

"Dr. Banner, listen to me," said Scott calmly. "Once I was shrunk down and inside an empty beehive. I was surprised when the whole swarm suddenly came back. It was terrifying. Bee stings hurt when you're normal size, but when you're tiny, they can easily kill you."

Ant-Man paused for a second. Was Banner listening?

"Bees can smell fear," Ant-Man continued. "And if that swarm had smelled my fear pheromones, they would have attacked me. If I wanted to stay alive, I had to stay calm enough not to give off the scent of fear in my sweat. By focusing on how I would feel once I was out, I was able to control my fear for hours, until the Pym Particles wore off and I went back to normal size."

Now Banner's breathing seemed more normal, like he was back in control.

"If I could do it, you can, too, Dr. Banner," Ant-Man finished.

"It's time you start calling me Bruce, Scott," Banner said calmly.

Anger-free, Banner struggled through the white blood cells and implanted the cure in one of the floating zombie viruses nearby.

"You did it!" shouted Scott, capturing the data that rolled in. "We have what we need to mass-produce the cure!"

But then the lab door burst open and in poured a team of **S.H.I.E.L.D.** agents . . . a team of infected, living undead **S.H.I.E.L.D.** agents!

CHAPTER 8

"I'll take left, you take right!" Cap shouted to Hawkeye as he sprang forward.

Hawkeye instantly obeyed Cap's order, leaping into action by his side. The two were a blur of activity, knocking out one zombified **S.H.I.E.L.D.** agent after another!

But there were just too many of them! Living undead agents slipped past Cap and Hawkeye and instantly ran toward Ant-Man.

"I've still got to get Bruce out of there!" Ant-Man shouted to the others as he dodged the snapping jaws of the agents who came at him.

"Do it as quickly as you can, soldier!" Cap shouted back to him.

Between Ant-Man and Tony Stark's body, where Banner was still trapped, were five snarling and growling undead!

"Here goes nothing," Ant-Man said as he flung himself at the undead. In midair, he shrank. The shrinking moved him out of the way of some grasping zombie hands! Ant-Man quickly shrank or grew to different sizes as needed to dodge the arms of the agents who desperately snatched at him.

"*MOVE IT*, Ant-Man!" shouted Hawkeye as he knocked out two more of the agents. "We can't keep this up forever!"

Finally reaching the table where Tony Stark was lying, Ant-Man shrank down and ran across the surface, grabbing the device needed to extract Banner.

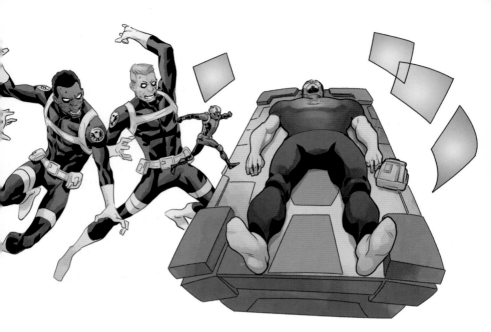

"Hold on, Bruce!" shouted Ant-Man into his comm. "You're coming out, but we've got company."

Using the device, Ant-Man withdrew Banner from Tony's body, then hit him with **Pym Particles**. Banner grew to normal size next to Ant-Man. Ant-Man, too, returned to his usual height.

"That's what you mean by company?" Banner asked, seeing the **S.H.I.E.L.D.** undead advancing.

"Let's draw them away from Tony's unconscious body!" Ant-Man said, grabbing Bruce and pulling him towards the door, where Cap and Hawkeye were trying to make a path for them to get through.

At exactly that moment, Ant-Man's comms carried a message from Falcon. "Ant-Man, are you there?" Falcon asked.

"In the middle of something," Ant-Man answered, still pulling Banner through the room crowded with living undead.

"Fine—but we need that cure now!" Falcon replied. **"We just lost Black Widow to the undead team."**

Out in the street, Falcon and Thor were trying to push back a horde of living undead that was attempting to enter an apartment building filled with uninfected people. Euclid was still with them, bucking and knocking down rows of zombies, but there were just too many of them.

"The cure is developed! We'll get it out to you as soon as we can!" Ant-Man promised Falcon. "But we have to get ourselves out of here first! It looks like the whole population of the Helicarrier has become infected!"

Ant-Man and Banner were now only a few feet away from Cap and Hawkeye, who had cleared a zombie-free path down the corridor to freedom.

"We're counting on you," Falcon called. **"Stay safe!"**

"We will!" shouted Banner, when suddenly a group of infected **S.H.I.E.L.D.** agents broke past Cap and slammed into Ant-Man

and Banner, knocking them to the ground.

"Or maybe we won't!" said Ant-Man as the living undead fell on them.

"No!" Banner screamed as one of the living undead bit him. **"They got me!"**

CHAPTER 9

Ant-Man pushed the living undead away from them, reaching out to Banner, who had just been bitten.

"I'm. . .already starting. . .to feel the change," Banner said as blue veins began to bulge out of his skin.

"Bruce, no!" cried Ant-Man as he kicked back more infected agents.

"It was great . . . working with you . . . Scott," said Banner.

"No, this can't be how it ends!" shouted Ant-Man.

"Oh, I don't think it will be," came a voice from the other side of the room.

Ant-Man and Banner looked past the crowd of zombies on top of them to see Tony Stark getting up from the lab table.

"The cure works!" shouted Ant-Man, a smile leaping to his face. "Iron Man's back with us!"

"Armour, to me!" Tony shouted.

Within seconds, pieces of the Iron Man suit flew through the door past Cap and Hawkeye.

"What a beautiful sight," said Hawkeye as the Iron Man helmet zoomed by.

Piece by piece, the armour slammed onto Tony Stark's body. In the blink of an eye, Tony had become the **Incredible Iron Man!**

"These **S.H.I.E.L.D.** agents have terrible people skills," Iron Man joked. "Let's teach them some manners!"

BAM-BAM!

Iron Man blasted the living undead around Ant-Man and Banner. The zombies went flying, landing unconscious nearby. Ant-Man was no longer cornered!

He ran to the lab table and grabbed some of the cure that had just been tested on Iron Man. "This will do the job, Bruce," he said, injecting Banner.

"That was . . . as close as they come . . ." said Banner, his skin already turning back to normal.

Nearby, Iron Man blasted more of the S.H.I.E.L.D. agents.

"Don't worry," Iron Man called out. "I'm using the stun setting on these guys. They're good agents, and I want them to have a chance to get back to normal, just like I did."

"Thank you for saving us, Tony!" said a relieved Ant-Man.

"Well, the memories of my time as a member of the living undead aren't very clear," said Iron Man, "but I can tell that I must owe you and Bruce a favour or two, Ant-Man. And I had this crazy dream that a mini Hulk was in my bloodstream."

"Some dream..." said Banner, his voice trailing off.

Iron Man looked confused for a second, then shrugged, saying, "Well, whatever you did, since I'm back to my handsome self, I take it you were able to create an effective **cure**?"

"We did," Ant-Man confirmed, "and thanks to data we received by testing it on you, we can turn the cure into a medical **mist**. It will turn the infected back to normal just by being sprayed on them."

"What do you need from me?" asked Iron Man.

"For now, if you could keep any more infected people from making it into the lab, that would be enough," explained Banner. "We just need time to make the mist."

"Consider it done!" said Iron Man as he zipped off to help Cap and Hawkeye fight.

Ant-Man and Banner immediately began programming the lab's medical equipment to produce as much of the cure in mist form as possible.

"Let's load the mist into canisters," Ant-Man suggested. "We'll create as much as we can before we run out of raw materials."

With Cap, Hawkeye and Iron Man all working together, they had no problem keeping the infected **S.H.I.E.L.D.** agents out of the lab. It wasn't long before Ant-Man and Banner had created a stockpile of medical mist.

"That's all we can make for now," Ant-Man said, looking over the canisters. "Let's get this out to the streets and **hope it's enough**."

Soon Ant-Man and the other Avengers were spraying the medical mist on the crowds of living undead walking the streets of New York. Within seconds, the citizens started transforming back to normal, shaking their heads in confusion, as if they were waking from a dream.

"It's working!" said Falcon happily as he sprayed Black Widow, returning her to normal.

Hawkeye had loaded the medical mist into his gas arrows and was firing them left and right into crowds of living undead. As the arrowheads popped, the gas sprayed out and cured large groups of people.

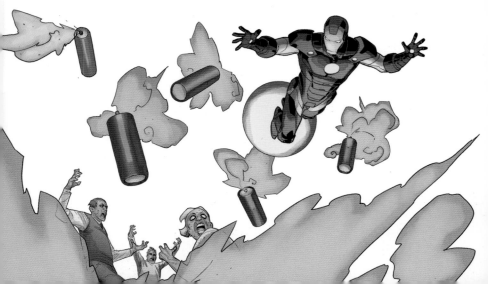

Iron Man was flying over alleys packed with living undead, swooping in low and opening the canisters so that the mist spread over everyone. "I feel like I've turned into a crop duster," Iron Man joked.

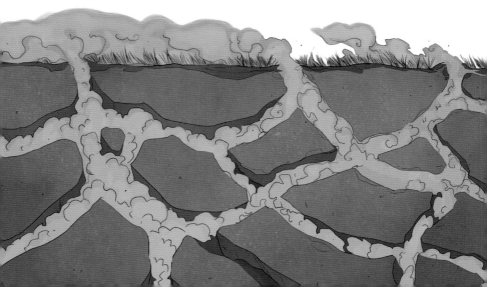

Thor threw a canister into Central Park, zapping it with a bolt of lightning and creating a mist shower. "There!" shouted Thor. "Now Ant-Man's insect comrades will also be relieved of the sickness!"

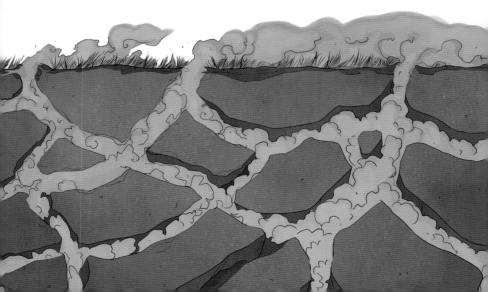

The plan was working, but when Ant-Man and Banner checked out the remaining supply of mist, they realised they were running low.

"We can't run out of mist before we cure everyone," Ant-Man said. "If even one zombie is still out there, it'll infect more, and this will all start over again."

Banner nodded. "If only there was a way to get all of the remaining undead in one central place so that we could use the mist that's left to cure everyone at the same time."

"But how? What would draw them all together?" Ant-Man wondered out loud.

"They want to bite more people, so maybe we could use ourselves as bait," suggested Banner. "Get them to follow us somewhere that we can trap them."

"It's a good idea, but there are people all over the city that they could bite. Why would they be drawn to us?" Ant-Man replied. "We have to try something else. If we can't draw them out...then maybe..."

Suddenly, Ant-Man remembered something Banner had told him earlier in the day...and it gave him an idea he thought just might work.

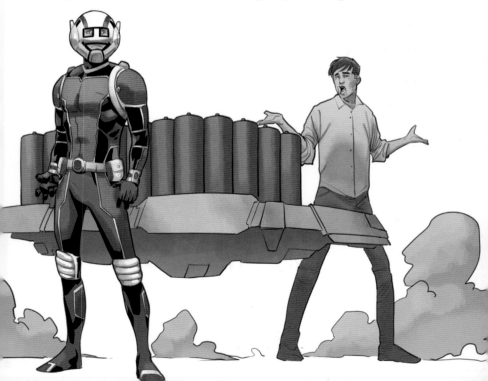

"*A*re you sure about this?" asked a sceptical Banner when he heard Ant-Man's plan.

"Not really," admitted Ant-Man. "However, I can't think of anything else."

"But we've been trying to stop me from turning into the Hulk all day," Banner pointed out.

Ant-Man's idea was simple. "When we were talking earlier, and you were telling me how the Hulk is often misunderstood, you said, **'Everything runs from the Hulk,'**" Ant-Man explained. "I get why that's normally a problem, but now we can turn it into a strength."

Banner had to admit that Ant-Man was right: the living undead would attack everything that moved, trying to bite and pass on their infection . . . but if anything could get them to run, it would be a rampaging Hulk.

"Okay, but if the Hulk winds up busting up the city, I'm telling the mayor it was your fault," said Banner.

Banner nervously walked straight into a crowd of the living undead. It was easy for the scientist to let himself grow angry as the infected grabbed at him and tried to bite. Moments later Banner's body started to grow and turn green.

His body mass doubled, then tripled, then quadrupled. By the time the transformation was complete, nothing recognisable was left of Banner. Instead, there was just . . . **the Incredible Hulk!**

The Hulk roared and all the living undead around him stopped advancing for a second. Even the sound of him was giving them pause. **"Hey, Hulk!"** shouted Ant-Man, shrinking and jumping onto his shoulder. "Can you hear me?"

Hulk looked at Ant-Man. "Little man Hulk's friend?" the green goliath asked.

"Yes, but you see the zombie people? You have to chase them to this place." Ant-Man used a holo-projector to show Hulk a picture of

Madison Square Garden, an arena big enough to hold all the remaining living undead.

"Hulk just smash zombie people?" Hulk suggested with a roar.

"No, the zombie people are Hulk's friends, too," Ant-Man answered quickly. "They're just sick. Round them up, okay?"

"Okay," said Hulk. **"Hulk like chase!"**

And with that, he was off!

Ant-Man's plan worked like a charm. When the living undead saw Hulk coming, they ran as fast as their diseased zombie legs would carry them! It was just like Banner had said: everything ran from the Hulk.

"I was sceptical," said Iron Man to Ant-Man as he watched the Hulk chase the last of the remaining living undead into Madison Square Garden. **"But it looks like this is going to work."**

Black Widow and Thor helped load the remaining medical mist canisters into the building's ventilation system, opening them before sealing the outside vents shut. They expected the ventilation fans to spread the mist through the arena, delivering the cure to all inside.

"You spoke too soon, Iron Man," said Falcon, scanning the building. **"It's not working. The mist isn't circulating!"**

Inside, Ant-Man could see that some of the living undead were already banging on the now closed Madison Square Garden entrance. A crack started to spread across one of the glass doors. It wouldn't hold for long.

"I'm on it," said Ant-Man. "Just tell me where the blockage is, Falcon!"

"I can do better than tell you," said Falcon as he projected a 3D hologram from his handheld device. It featured a rotating image of the building's ventilation system, highlighting the problem spot in red.

Ant-Man studied the hologram for a second, looking at it with an eye for detail honed by hours spent poring over the schematics of electrical systems.

"Got it. Wish me luck!" Ant-Man said as he shrank down to ant size and slipped into the arena's air ducts.

He scurried through the ducts, growing and shrinking as needed to fit through the different corridors and quickly making it to the jammed fan indicated by Falcon's hologram.

"Found it," he said, giving the fan a push to try to start it moving again.

But it didn't work.

"It's not moving," Ant-Man said, trying again.

"Maybe it's not a simple jam after all," suggested Falcon over his comm.

Ant-Man looked around and spotted the electrical wires that fed into the fan's motor. He popped off an access hatch and searched around in the system.

"You're right, not a jam . . . we've got an electrical problem," Ant-Man announced. **"Good thing we've also got an electrical engineer!"**

Ant-Man patched together two wires. He knew instantly that it had worked.

"Gotcha!" Ant-Man shouted as the air flowed past him.

As the mist circulated through the system and started to cure the remaining infected New Yorkers, Ant-Man jumped back out of the air vent and sized up. All the Avengers cheered and gathered around him.

"Tiny man now less tiny," observed a confused Hulk.

"I have to admit, you did great today," Hawkeye said to Ant-Man.

"And we owe you an apology," said Falcon. "If we had taken you more seriously right away, things would never have gotten this bad."

"That's not a mistake we'll make again," Cap stated.

"Definitely not," agreed Black Widow.

Ant-Man smiled. "Thanks, everybody," he said. "That means a lot coming from Earth's Mightiest Heroes!"

Later, after Hulk had calmed down and turned back into Banner, Ant-Man got a message to meet the doctor in his Helicarrier lab.

"Hey, Bruce, what's up?" asked Scott when he walked in.

"Nothing. I needed you here so you could get a **S.H.I.E.L.D.** security pass to our lab," said Banner.

Scott didn't think he'd heard that right. **"*Our* lab?"**

"Yep," said Banner. "You can't do all

your scientific work in an anthill, so I hope you'll join me here from time to time."

"Are you sure?" asked Scott. "I mean, I'm not sure the other Avengers would want me around . . . "

"You're right," said Iron Man, entering the lab. "I usually don't like having competition in the genius department . . . but in your case, I'll make an exception."

"Genius?" asked Scott, surprised.

"What else would you call the guy who cured me, and half of New York, even after all the other so-called heroes had written him off?" asked Iron Man.

Ant-Man smiled from ear to ear.

"So what do you say?" asked Bruce. **"Lab partners?"**